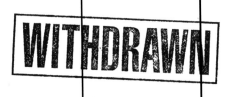

To all the Princess Boys in the world: you are loved.

Thank you for teaching us how to appreciate your uniqueness.

To Dean, Dkobe, and Dyson; you have my heart. —C. K.

ALADDIN

An imprint of Simon & Schuster Children's Publishing Division

1230 Avenue of the Americas, New York, NY 10020

First Aladdin hardcover edition December 2010

Text and illustrations copyright © 2009 by KD Talent LLC

All rights reserved, including the right of reproduction in whole or in part in any form.

ALADDIN is a trademark of Simon & Schuster, Inc., and related logo is a registered trademark of Simon & Schuster, Inc.

For information about special discounts for bulk purchases, please contact Simon & Schuster Special Sales at 1-866-506-1949 or business@simonandschuster.com.

The Simon & Schuster Speakers Bureau can bring authors to your live event. For more information or to book an event contact the Simon & Schuster Speakers Bureau at 1-866-248-3049 or visit our website at www.simonspeakers.com.

The text of this book was set in Minion Pro Regular.

Manufactured in China 0318 SCP

10

This book has been cataloged with the Library of Congress.

ISBN 978-1-4424-2988-8 (hc.)

ISBN 978-1-4424-3063-1 (eBook)

My Princess Boy™

As a community, we can accept and support
our children for whomever they are
and however they wish to look.

By Cheryl Kilodavis
Illustrated by Suzanne DeSimone

Aladdin
NEW YORK   LONDON   TORONTO   SYDNEY

My Princess Boy is four years old.

He likes pretty things.

Pink is his favorite color.

He plays dress up in girly dresses.

He dances like a beautiful ballerina.

My Princess Boy has a cool brother.
His brother plays baseball and soccer.
And his brother dances with my Princess Boy.
My Princess Boy loves his brother.

My Princess Boy loves his dad.

His dad tells my Princess Boy how pretty he looks in a dress.

His dad holds his hand and tells him to twirl!

My Princess Boy smiles and hugs his dad.

My Princess Boy has playdates with boys and girls.
He likes to climb trees in his Princess Boy tiara crown.

When he plays dress up, he likes to change clothes a lot.
He wears a green ballet leotard and dances with his friends.

I love my Princess Boy.
When we go shopping he is the happiest
when looking at girls' clothes.

But when he says he wants to buy a pink bag
or a sparkly dress, people stare at him.

And when he buys girl things, they laugh at him, and then they laugh at me.

It hurts us both.

Once my Princess Boy wore a dress
at his birthday party.

He welcomed his friends to his home and he said,
"I am a Princess Boy!"

He put on jewelry and he liked how pretty he looked
. . . and waved his Princess Boy wand.

And then my Princess Boy was
a princess for Halloween.
He went trick-or-treating with his brother.
One woman laughed at him because
he was in a princess dress.

My Princess Boy asked, "Why did she laugh at me?"

I told him some people don't think boys should wear dresses.

But a Princess Boy can wear a dress at his school and I will not laugh at him.

And a Princess Boy can wear pink and I will tell him how pretty he looks.

A Princess Boy can play with me in pretty girl clothes and I will still play with him.

If you see a Princess Boy . . .

Will you laugh at him?

Will you call him a name?

Will you play with him?

Will you like him for who he is?

Our Princess Boy is happy because we love him for who he is.

My Princess Boy

is your Princess Boy.